Hematite

Hornblende

Olivine

Limonite

Quartz

Silver

Pyroxene

Sulfur

Tourmaline

Berto
Yosemite's
Rock-Lovin' Bear

Remember!

Only bears are allowed to collect rocks in Yosemite!

By Marian Parks

Illustrated by Christine Karron

Yosemite National Park
Yosemite, California

North Dome

Washington
Column

Lehamite Falls

Royal Arches

Upper Yosemite Fall

Visitor Center

Lower Yosemite Fall

Eagle Peak

Three Brothers

Middle Brother

Sentin

Lower Brother

El Capitan

Black bears are gutsy, self-assured mountaineers,
Who climb steep granite rocks without worries or fears.
But Berto was different. He was ghastly afraid
Of climbing the cliffs where other bears played.

He stayed in the valley and daydreamed on walks
That one day he'd also scale Yosemite's rocks.
Surrounded by stones since the time of his birth,
Berto loved every rock that popped up from the earth.

Each day he'd seek favorite places to roam
And carry a load of rock specimens home.
He sorted his rocks, then grouped his collection
Into three rock types and labeled each section.

Permit to
Collect
Rocks

Sedimentary stones he'd found far away
In caves and in quarries out west near the bay.
He had limestone and coal, chert, sandstone, and shale,
Along with an ancient and fossilized snail.

The second rock group, the igneous rocks,
He collected at bases of cliffs on his walks.
His gabbro and granite had formed long ago
From magma that cooled in the earth far below.

Other igneous rocks cool fast above ground
When volcanoes erupt and spew lava around.
He'd found basalt and obsidian, too,
Far east of the park on a trail that he knew.

The third group of rocks was unique, even strange.
Heat and pressure had caused these odd stones to change.
These metamorphic rocks he found close to North Dome.
He used slate and quartzite to landscape his home.

DIORITE

OBSIDIAN

SLATE

QUARTZITE

GNEISS

METAMORPHIC

One day, while he searched near a small dogwood tree,
A rock hit his rump like a mad stinging bee.
"Put that in your rock heap!" a taunting voice cried.
Berto knew it was Buck, so he ran home to hide.

Buck was a bully, a misguided brute,
Who liked kicking rocks down the Glacier Point chute.
Buck's bad behavior had grown more severe,
And Berto ranked Buck as his number one fear.

Berto hid in his cave for most of the day
And timidly waited 'til Buck went away.
He peeked to make sure Buck was far out of sight
Before he departed for campfire night.

Bears aren't allowed at the ranger led show,
So he hid in the trees near the Fen Meadow.
Soft music wafted with a fun, folksy beat.
Berto sang along and tapped his big feet.

The crowd became quiet as the ranger began
To retell the legend of a famous park man.
"John Muir was a leader, a park pioneer,
A wise naturalist, and a brave mountaineer.

"He studied the valley and plant conservation
And led a fierce fight for land preservation.
Muir met each challenge with courage and might.
He ignored his fears to do what was right.

"'Go to the mountains,' John Muir liked to say.
He adored those rocks nature put on display."
"John Muir is my hero," Berto whispered aloud
And then hit the trail home, avoiding the crowd.

When Berto got home he knew right away
That he'd been a victim of wicked foul play!
His cave had been ransacked; rocks were strewn all about.
That Buck was the culprit Berto had no doubt!

Berto's sorrowful cry echoed off the cliff walls
From the mighty El Cap to the Nevada Falls.
Berto stomped his broad feet, and he yanked at his hair.
He wished he had the guts to confront that mean bear.

IGNEOUS

EDIMENTARY

METAMORPHIC

He thought of revenge—a get-even scheme—
But instead walked along the Merced River stream.
He tossed a few pebbles, watched them plop and then sink.
He needed some time to calm down and to think.

The minerals gleamed, crystals catching the light.
The quartz twinkled next to the dark biotite.
Berto remembered what a ranger once said:
"These rocks tumbled down from the cliffs overhead.

"These rocks may have traveled with an old glacier flow
That carved out this valley a long time ago.
The glacial ice ground at Yosemite's stone,
Exposing granite much tougher than bone."

"I need to get tough like these rocks," Berto said.
And then Buck appeared just a few feet ahead.
"Get lost," Buck yelled, with a blood-chilling stare,
But Berto glared back at the bullying bear.

Berto rose to full height. His nostrils flared out.
He growled from his throat and puffed from his snout.
His eyes were ablaze like a fire at night.
Then Buck turned around and lumbered out of sight.

Berto rarely saw Buck. They both stayed away
From each other until one frightful, grim day.
Berto was near Mirror Lake, heading home,
And noticed a ruckus on top of Half Dome.

As he walked further south, crossing Tenaya Creek,
He heard a loud cry, a bloodcurdling shriek:
"Help! I'm afraid. Please, help me, I'm stuck!"
This time it was clear that the victim was Buck.

When Berto got home he could see Glacier Point
And Buck, who was caught in a rock crevice joint.
Terrified, Buck hung suspended in air,
But nobody wanted to rescue that bear.

Berto thought of John Muir and right away knew
That a trip up the cliff was long overdue!
He cautiously stepped on the talus rock base
Focused and calm, he scaled the steep face.

Steady on his feet and relaxed in the knees,
Berto was surprised that he felt so at ease.
With each rising step his confidence grew.
He knew he'd succeed at the job he must do.

The former foes met, had a bear-to-bear talk
Before Berto agreed to free Buck from the rock.
Buck didn't bluster, act rudely or tough,
And he promised to end all the bullying stuff.

Berto kept climbing to Glacier Point's crest.
He gazed at the cliffs soaring north, east, and west.
Waterfalls thundered, granite glittered and danced.
The rocks celebrated. The bears were entranced.

Half Dome rejoiced, and rocks rolled down its face,
Adding to the pile of stones at its base.
Yosemite's cliffs seemed to smile and say,
"Good for you, Berto, you were gutsy today."

In this tribute to Berto, the cliffs somehow knew
The dream of this rock-lovin' bear had come true.
Balanced on a rock three thousand feet in the air
Stood Berto, the proudest Yosemite bear!

For Steve, my partner in love, fun, and big ideas.

—M.P.

For Neal, Kida, and Jack. I'm a lucky mom.

—Ch.K.

Nature Tale Books, Inc.
Livermore, California
www.NatureTaleBooks.com
Sales@NatureTaleBooks.com

LCCN: 2016906530

Summary: A Yosemite black bear, who collects rocks,
overcomes his fears and gains confidence.

Story themes: Earth Science | Rocks | Bullying | Yosemite National Park | Bears

Hardcover ISBN: 978-1-943172-01-6

Illustrations were created in watercolor, acrylic, colored pencil,
and ink by Christine Karron.

Printed in USA

10 9 8 7 6 5 4 3 2 1

Nature Tale Books

Visit our website for
Common Core Activities
www.NatureTaleBooks.com